ROMEOSAURUS AND JULIET REX

by Mo O'Hara   illustrated by Andrew Joyner

HARPER
An Imprint of HarperCollinsPublishers

For Guy, Charlotte, and Daniel with love —M.O.

For Jane and Michael —A.J.

Romeosaurus and Juliet Rex

Text copyright © 2018 by Mo O'Hara

Illustrations copyright © 2018 by Andrew Joyner

All rights reserved. Manufactured in China.

No part of this book may be used or reproduced in any manner whatsoever without written permission
except in the case of brief quotations embodied in critical articles and reviews. For information address
HarperCollins Children's Books, a division of HarperCollins Publishers, 195 Broadway, New York, NY 10007.

www.harpercollinschildrens.com

ISBN 978-0-06-265274-4

The artist used Procreate and Adobe Photoshop to create the digital illustrations for this book.

Typography by Chelsea C. Donaldson

18 19 20 21 22 SCP 10 9 8 7 6 5 4 3 2 1

❖

First Edition

Once upon a time, one hundred and fifty million years ago, two families, both alike in lizardness, lived in the swampland of Verona.

Romeosaurus's family were herbivores.
"Yaaaaaaay! Ferns for dinner! Yaaaaaaaay!"

Juliet Rex's family were carnivores.
"Yaaaaaay! Herbivores for dinner! Yaaaaaay!"

You can see why the families didn't really get along.

One day Juliet Rex was stomping through the swampland on her way to the Dinosaur Ball.

"Do my arms look small in this?" she asked her nanny, Nurse-a-Dactyl.

"Of course, dear," Nurse-a-Dactyl answered.

Meanwhile Romeosaurus was clomping along with his
friend Mercutio-tops on his way to crash the ball. Now,
usually when a stegosaurus and a triceratops "crash" a ball,
you would know it, but this time they went in disguise,
because it was a masked ball, for carnivores only.

The carnivores really knew how to throw a party, and Juliet Rex was waving her tiny arms in the air like she just didn't care when she spotted a dinosaur who she had never seen before.

He swished his tail at her to say hello. She thumped her tail back to say, "I might be casually waving hi or I might just be swatting a prehistoric bug. Your call."

Romeosaurus went over,
and the two dinos danced.

They giggled, they talked,
they played, and they
started to become friends.

"Do you want to get something
to eat?" Juliet Rex asked as she
led Romeosaurus over to the
buffet.

"AUNTIE GLADYS!!" Romeosaurus gulped.

Romeosaurus rushed to help Auntie Gladys off the buffet table and take the apple out of her mouth.

"Wait, you're a herbivore?" Juliet Rex asked, taking off Romeosaurus's mask.

"And you're a carnivore."

Just then a fight broke out at the Dinosaur Ball. Apparently, Mercutio-tops had poked Juliet Rex's cousin, Tybalt Rex, with his horns while dancing.

"You'd better go," Juliet Rex said, sneaking Romeosaurus out during the commotion. "Will I see you again?" Romeosaurus looked back and smiled.

That night Juliet Rex looked out from her clifftop balcony.

"Romeosaurus, Romeosaurus. Wherefore art thou Romeosaurus?"

"Pssst. Down here," Romeosaurus answered. "Stegosauruses aren't very good at climbing. It's the tail, really, and the weight, and the complete lack of claws to grip anything, and—"

"There's a stone ramp over there," Juliet Rex interrupted.

"Oh, thanks."

Once again they giggled and played and talked and laughed, and they became true friends.

"My family would never want me to be friends with you," Juliet Rex said. "I mean, I could never invite you over for dinner. You would be the main course."

"My family wouldn't like it either. Especially Auntie Gladys," Romeosaurus said, sighing.

"Then what can we do?" Juliet Rex wondered.

When Nurse-a-Dactyl woke the next morning, she found that
Juliet Rex's bed had not been slept in. And she found a note.

A herbivore is my true friend.
So off I go to swampland's end.

Nurse-a-Dactyl flew down to the herbivores'
home and tapped her talon on the door.
Auntie Gladys answered.
"AAAAAAAAAAHHHHHHHHHHHHH!"
she screamed, and then fainted.

Mercutio-tops pulled Auntie Gladys out of the way. Nurse-a-Dactyl showed him Juliet Rex's note, and he showed her the note Romeosaurus had left for him.

You have always been a friend to me.
But a carnivore has set my heart free.

Nurse-a-Dactyl made a face.
"They're not very good at poetry, but
they do seem to care a lot about each
other, even though they're so different."

"They have bad poetry in common,
I guess," Mercutio-tops added.

"We need to find them. They're
headed for the tar pits, and that's
dangerous for any dinosaur,
herbivore or carnivore." Nurse-a-
Dactyl flapped her wings . . .

. . . and carried Mercutio-tops above the swampland until they reached the tar pits. They could see some things floating on the tar. It was Romeosaurus's feathered hat and Juliet Rex's backpack.

"We're too late!" shrieked Nurse-a-Dactyl.

"We should have let them be friends!" Mercutio-tops cried.

"You're right," Nurse-a-Dactyl sobbed. "Then maybe they'd both still be here."

"But we *are* here," Juliet Rex said as she and Romeosaurus came out from behind a boulder.

"My little dino!!!" Nurse-a-Dactyl gathered Juliet Rex in for a wingy hug. Mercutio-tops spluttered, "But your hat? The backpack?"

"We were just looking for a big stick to fish them out with when you both showed up," Romeosaurus said.

"So . . . can we be friends?" Juliet asked.

"And just to be clear, carnivore friends don't eat other friends, right?" Romeosaurus added.

"I could never eat a true friend of my darling Juliet Rex," Nurse-a-Dactyl said. Then she whispered to Romeosaurus, "but if you break her heart, you're in a sandwich by lunchtime—you got it?"

"So it's a deal. Carnivores and herbivores will be friends," Mercutio-tops said.
And they all shook hands on it.
Well, except for Juliet Rex, as hers wouldn't reach, but she nodded in agreement.

And they lived happily ever after.

Until...